Rhyme & PUNishment

ADVENTURES IN WORDPLAY

BY **Brian P. Cleary**

ILLUSTRATED BY **J. P. Sandy**

M MILLBROOK PRESS / MINNEAPOLIS

Millbrook Press
A division of Lerner Publishing Group
241 First Avenue North
Minneapolis, MN 55401 U.S.A.

Website address: www.lernerbooks.com

Library of Congress Cataloging-in-Publication Data

Cleary, Brian P., 1959—
    Rhyme and punishment : adventures in wordplay / by Brian P. Cleary ;
illustrated by J. P. Sandy.
        p.   cm.
    ISBN-13: 978-1-57505-849-8 (lib. bdg. : alk. paper)
    ISBN-10: 1-57505-849-9 (lib. bdg. : alk. paper)
    1. Children's poetry, American. 2. Puns and punning—Juvenile literature.
I. Sandy, J. P. II. Title.
PS3553.L39144R49 2006
811'.54—dc22   2003004517

Manufactured in the United States of America
1 2 3 4 5 6 – DP – 11 10 09 08 07 06

To my sister, Liz
—B. P. C.

To Joyce, Eric, and Michael
—J. P. S.

What is a PUN?

A pun is a little verbal joke—a "twist" or a "play" on words. The simplest puns sound like a word of similar pronunciation but different spelling. When people realize that the word can be heard or understood in two different ways, it makes them laugh and sometimes roll their eyes and groan, as in this one:

Seven days without ice cream makes one **weak**.

Are you able to see the wordplay, or pun, in that sentence?

A more complex type of pun involves a word that sounds like a whole phrase or part of a phrase, as in "**Jamaica** sandwich?" What five-word sentence does that phrase sound like? If you guessed, "**Did you make a** sandwich?" then you're thinking punny already! See how you magically turned two words into five by hearing them differently? What is the pun or word joke in the phrase, "Give me **Bach** my **Schubert**"? That's right: "Give me **back** my **shoe, Bert**."

Puns are more common than you think.

They are usually the star feature in a knock-knock joke, like this one:

Knock, knock!

   Who's there?

Wendy.

   Wendy who?

Wendy ya think we'll eat? I'm hungry!

Sometimes you bump into a pun by accident. Once when I was in 5th grade, our teacher was commenting on a car horn we'd heard from the parking lot. It had an unusual sound, so she said, "Somebody has a unique horn out there." What I heard was "Somebody has a unicorn out there."

Puns often stretch or bend the pronunciation of a word for the sake of a laugh. If you're having trouble figuring out a pun, just stop and sound out the syllables in front of you, asking yourself, "what other word does this sound like?" Sometimes it helps to say the word or phrase out loud. Often you will uncover the pun right there. When I was young, I tried to uncover puns by using what I now know is called context. That means I looked carefully at the words surrounding the pun and tried to place a word or phrase that would logically make sense there, sounding something like the word or phrase I was trying to decode. It also helps to write out the phrase on paper like this:

You never SAUSAGE love.

To figure this out, you can list words that look or sound a little like the pun. (For instance, "sauce itch" doesn't make sense, but "saw such" does.) You can also figure out a pun by reading a sentence quickly or trying to emphasize different syllables. As you're reading this book, if you come across a word that you've never seen before or that you're not sure how to pronounce, look to the bottom of the page for my handy "pun-unciation" guide, then sound it out.

When I set out to write the puns in this book, I read books on each topic (like animals and geography) and made a list of the words that sound like other words and phrases. For example, in the geography section, I saw the word "Cuba" on a map, and I wrote in my notes "Cuba sugar," because it sounds like "cube of sugar."

Once you learn the trick of figuring out puns, try making up a few yourself. If you try one out on your dad or your teacher and you get a loud groan, you know you've got a good one!

Let the
PUNishment begin ...

Brian P. Cleary

MUSIC

{Going for **Baroque**}

My buddy Bert likes **Haydn** things—
he's sometimes hard to **Handel**.
I said, "Give me **Bach** my **Schubert**,"
'cause I knew he hid my sandal.

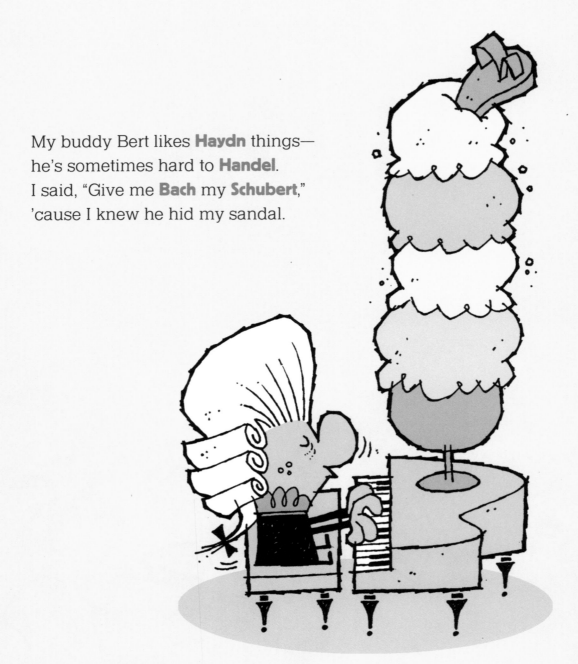

Haydn *(HY-den) is the last name of the Austrian classical music composer Franz Joseph Haydn, who lived from 1732 to 1809.*

Handel *and* **Bach** *(rhymes with "rock") are the last names of George Frideric Handel and Johann Sebastian Bach, two composers who were born in Germany in the very same year, 1685.*

Schubert *(SHOO-bert) is the last name of the Austrian composer Franz Schubert, who played violin and piano. He lived from 1797 to 1828.*

My friend Ray borrows books to **reed** and balls to **pitch** and throw. I keep good **notes**, and **sol fa re** owes **mi** a **la ti do**.

"**Accordion** to my **records**," I told him, "you still owe my mom a **tuba** toothpaste. How can you **sing solo**?"

---

reed *is the vibrating part of the mouthpiece on some wind instruments, like the clarinet.*
pitch *refers to the highness or lowness of a sound.*
do, re, mi, fa, sol, la, *and* **ti** *are notes on the major scale. To get the puns, you need to know that these words are pronounced like "doh," "ray," "mee," "fah," "soh," "lah," and "tee."*
solo *is a musical term that means to sing or play an instrument by oneself.*

When it comes to kicking field goals,
you just can't **beat** Tom's toes.
Yes, anyone with his **legato**
duet in the pros.

---

legato *(lih-GAH-toh) is a musical term that means smooth or flowing. The pun phrase that it's supposed to sound like is three words long.*
duet *(doo-ET) is a performance by two instrumentalists or two singers.*

Could rain deter his distance? No!
Woodwind blow out his fire?
If I said he's not **A natural**,
I guess I'd be a **lyre**.

A natural ("A" sounds like "ay") is the note that orchestras tune their instruments to.
lyre (rhymes with "tire") is an ancient stringed-instrument.

When crossing streets she warns us,
"There could be **A-major** loss,
'cause if you don't **C-sharp**, you could
B-flat before you cross!"

A-major, C-sharp, and **B-flat** are all musical notes. They also each have scales named after them.

"You'll be sprawled across the blacktop—
it's **cymbal** as can be—
and you'll **guitar** all over you!
So listen—that's the **key**!"

My uncle **Waltz** a shepherd,
and his flock is down to half.
He needs some help to keep his sheep,
and so he'll get a **staff**.

Walt fished for **tenor** 12 years,
but it made **hymn** too upset.
"If they got away, you starved—
if you reeled 'em **minuet**."

staff *refers to the five parallel lines on which musical notes are placed to indicate pitch.*
tenor *(TEH-nehr) is the highest natural adult male voice.*
hymn *(HIM) is a religious song of praise or joy.*
minuet *(MIN-yoo-ET) is the music for a slow stately dance for two.*

My friends the twins look so alike
that some **chimes** I forget—
I often think Annette is Claire,
or I'll call **Clarinet**.

They **tune** into the older films
and love to watch the dancing.
"There's too much **sax** and **violins** now,
and not enough romancing."

I always pick the scary films—
the dark, grotesque, and gory.
They often make me **fret** at night,
but that's **sonata** story.

fret *refers to those bars or ridges on the fingerboard of some stringed instruments, like the guitar or banjo, which help musicians place their fingers correctly to make particular notes.*
sonata *(seh-NAH-teh) is a composition for one or two instruments, often in several different movements.*

ANIMALS

{Laugh Until You're **Horse**}

My dad predicts the weather,
and he **toad** my sister once,
"It looks a lot like **reindeer**,
so be sure to wear your pumps."

My sister Mary travels some
to **Filly**, Frankfurt, Rome.
And though she's never gone for long,
it's nice when **Mare** comes home.

---

filly and **mare** *are both female horses. To get the pun here, you must know that "filly" and "mare" are short for other words. One is a city in Pennsylvania, and the other is a girl's name.*

I **gopher** stays at Grandpa's house—
wolf fish and **yak** till dawn.
"My fishing isn't bad," he says,
"but, lord, my **herring**'s gone."

yak *is a long-haired animal in the ox family that is found in Tibet and other parts of central Asia.*
herring *is a soft-finned fish.*

My brother Sam plays baseball—
he's a **raven loon** at **bat**.
And if they're **pigeon** him inside,
he doesn't **swallow** that.

He'll **fowl** 'em off on **porpoise**,
saying, "**Toucan** play this game."
And then he'll end up **bunting**—
it's a single just the same.

---

loon *is a large bird that feeds on fish.*
swallow *(SWAH-loh) is a small bird that feeds on insects.*
bunting *is a stout-billed bird that is often a brilliant shade of blue.*

When **salmon** I go fishing,
we **horse** around and play.
Then **eel** always end up **lion**
'bout the ones that got away.

salmon *(SA-mehn) is an anadromous fish, which means it swims upstream from the sea for breeding.*
eel *is a long, bony, snakelike fish with slimy skin.*

I eat the same lunch every day
(I won't try something **gnu**):
a ham on **rhino** pickle
and a **parrot** Twinkies, too.

gnu (sounds like "new") is an interesting animal. Although its head is like that of an ox, it is a member of the African antelope family. Both the boy and girl have horns.
rhino (rhymes with "I know") is the shortened form of rhinoceros, an Asian and African mammal with little hair and one or two horns on its snout. Separate the first and second syllable to get the pun here.

My grandma wears a two-foot wig
that's held on with **ape** pin.
But if you think her hair is big,
ewe otter sea urchin.

Although she's funny looking,
she's **deer** as she can be.
When once I asked her for some **doe**,
she gave a **buck** to me!"

---

ewe *(YOO) is a female sheep.*
otter *is an aquatic mammal (it looks similar to a weasel or mink) and has claws and webbed feet.*
sea urchin *is related to the starfish and is one of the favorite meals of otters.*
deer, doe, *and* **buck** *are all related. A doe is a female deer, and a buck is a male deer.*

Our cat is kind **dove shellfish**
and thinks the world is hers.
She finds a comfy spot, and then
we pet **turtle sheep** purrs.

shellfish *is an invertebrate, which means it does not have a spinal column.*
As the name suggests, it's a water-dwelling animal with a shell.

One Saturday my mom
asked me to help **piranha** quest.
She **smelt** a mouse inside the house
but couldn't find the pest.

We searched about the kitchen
from our **perch** atop a chair,
till we discovered what she
smelled was **moose** upon her **hare**.

piranha *(pih-RAH-nuh) is a brightly colored South American fish with sharp teeth. It may attack large mammals (including humans!).*
smelt *is a fish that's similar to salmon. What past-tense verb does smelt sort of sound like?*
perch *is a bony freshwater fish.*

When it's **stork**, I think about
my family, and I roar:
"We could be a lot more normal,
but **owl** bet we'd be a **boar**!"

ROWRR!

boar *is a male in the swine (which is a fancy word for pig) family.*

FOOD

{The **Wurst** Puns
You've Ever Heard}

My folks are Hank and Margie,
and you never **sausage** love.
He tells her, "**Margarine** my **sole**—
you're **roll** I'm dreaming of!"

sole *is a small-mouthed fish.*

He spent his youth be **cider**
and one **thyme** said in fun,
"I don't know why we **cantaloupe**—
we're **olive** twenty-one!"

thyme *(sounds like "time") is an herb that is used to season foods. You'll find thyme growing mostly in Spain, France, and Portugal.*
cantaloupe *(KAN-tuh-lohp) is a type of melon with orange flesh that's high in vitamin C. To decode the pun, you may need to look up the word "elope" in a dictionary.*

Their song was on the radio,
a **sherbet** sign, she felt.
"He knew that I'd say yes, 'cause
when they play that **tuna melt**."

sherbet *is an icy fruit-flavored dessert (kind of like ice cream).*

They **honey**mooned in Paris,
bounced checks without concern.
It'll be a long, long time **beef** for
the **French toast** their return!

The **pear** moved in with Mother's folks and didn't have **mushroom**.
So they started **pudding dough** a **whey** to buy a farm in June.

pudding is a sweet, creamy treat. Folks from England also make it out of corn, oatmeal, sausage, or even kidney!

whey (WAY) is the watery-colored milky liquid that is removed from the curd when cheese is made. Remember Little Miss Muffet? She was busy eating some curds and whey.

Now they're **raisin** kids and crops
and just one cow who's **beet**.
She might **beef fat** and tired,
buttermilk is rather sweet.

beet *is a plant with edible leaves and a purplish root that is a vegetable.*
buttermilk *is the liquid (or milk) that remains after butter is churned.*

My nana is as **Gouda** cook
as you will ever **meat**.
Cheese always **bacon** cookies,
and I **Edam** by the sheet.

Herb back is to the cookbook—
no measuring, no rules.
But a pie that's made **banana**
will be gone before it cools.

Gouda *(GOO-dah) is a mild type of cheese made in the Netherlands.*
Edam *(EE-dehm) is a yellow pressed cheese, also made in the Netherlands, that's usually round and has a red rind.*

We **relish** time together,
and we'll **pickle** little tune.
Icing and play the fiddle,
while Mom **jams** on bassoon.

relish *is often made from some combination of pickles, onions, tomatoes, and peppers and is added to plainer foods to give them more flavor. To understand the pun, you'll need to know that "relish" is also a verb.*

At nighttime **cold cuts** 'cross the plains
(it's **chili**, I'd **éclair**)—
but when the family's **salt** tucked in,
it warms the **dairy** air.

éclair *(ai-KLEHR) is a long, chocolate pastry that's filled with custard or cream.*

GEOGRAPHY

{Groan Until **Ukraine** Your Neck}

"**Jamaica Sandwich**?" Grandma asked,
and I replied, "I ate
some **Chile** from a **China** bowl
and **Turkey** from a plate."

I know my grandma's love **Israel**—
she told me as a lad,
"I'll feed you when you're **Hungary**,
Algeria when you're sad."

Sandwich *refers to "South Sandwich Islands," a group of islands in the southern Atlantic Ocean, near the tip of Argentina.*
Algeria *(al-JEER-ee-uh) is an African country. If you find Morocco, Mali, or Libya on a map, you're in the right neighborhood.*

"**U.S.** me how's your singing,"
said Aunt Anna as I bowed.
"**Juneau**, my boy, you **Singapore**,
but my, you sure sing loud!"

Aunt Anna can fix anything—
a **Paris** skates, a cup.
If your pants rip **Indonesia**
just **Havana** sew 'em up.

Juneau *(JOO-noh) is the capital of Alaska. Juneau can only be reached by air or water!*
Singapore *is near Malaysia and has four official languages: Chinese, Malay, Tamil, and English.*
Indonesia *(in-duh-NEE-zhuh) is a country in Southeast Asia. It's the world's largest archipelago, which means a group of scattered islands.*
Havana *is the capital of Cuba, which is off the southern tip of Florida.*

Iran and played at Grandpa's farm,
Greenland so plush and full—
I fed the pigs and milked the cows
and rode on **Istanbul**.

Istanbul *(IS-tan-bull) is the largest city in Turkey and used to be called Constantinople.*

As a **Syria** scholar of baseball,
my grandpa has often professed,
"Of all the men who ever played,
Beirut is still the best."

Syria *(SEER-ee-uh) is a Middle Eastern country near Israel and Lebanon.*
Beirut *(bay-ROOT) is the capital of Lebanon. What famous old-time baseball player does this city's name sound like?*

41

I **Russia** round on my red bike
and feel **New Zealand** vigor
when I take a kite and **Taiwan** on
and sail my ten-speed rigger.

Taiwan (ty-WAHN) *is an island located off the southeast coast of China.*

Burpin' and **Belgium** from root beer,
I made it come out of my nose.
Then I shook up a **Canada** stuff
and chugged it right down to my toes.

Belgium *(BEL-jehm) is a Dutch-, French-, and German-speaking country between France and Germany.*

My brother drank a **Malta** day
and dipped his fries in **Greece**.
And though his weight was **Dublin**,
his **Seoul** seemed quite at peace.

He started using **Sweden** low
and working off his belly.
But then the **Laos** got **Vatican**
when they opened that **New Delhi**.

Malta *is an island nation in southern Europe, near Italy.*
Dublin *(DUB-lin) is the capital of Ireland.*
Seoul *(SOLE) is the capital of South Korea and was home to the 1988 Summer Olympics.*
Laos *(rhymes with "mouse") is a country near China, Cambodia, and Thailand.*
Vatican *refers to "Vatican City," which is a country inside a country. It is the center of the Roman Catholic Church. Vatican City is home to only about 1,000 people, including the pope, and is located inside Rome, Italy.*

My dad comes home so tired
he can't keep his **Bering Strait**.
His **Sudan Thailand** on the floor,
his shoes land on his plate.

We went out to the racetrack,
Kenya tell why I'm upset?
I picked out all the winners,
but my dad's too cheap **Tibet**!

Bering Strait *is the narrow stretch of water that separates Alaska from Siberia.*
Sudan *(soo-DAHN) is on the east end of the Sahara near Egypt and Libya in Africa.*
Thailand *(rhymes with "my land") is a country near Laos, Cambodia, and Malaysia.*
Kenya *is a country in East Africa, on the coast of the Indian Ocean.*
Tibet *(tih-BEHT) is in southwest China and is home to some of the highest mountains in the world.*

"**Europe** too late," my grandma said.
"**Uganda** get some sleep.
Lie down in bed and count some **Wales**."
(I think that she meant sheep.)

Uganda *is a country near Sudan in Africa.*
Wales *is a hilly, mountainous region of Great Britain, where most people speak English or Welsh.*